WONDER GOAL!

pages from my sketchbooks— Michael Foreman

FUJI FOOTBALL   Japan 1996

NEW YORK   1997

Berlin Wall 1970

Siena, Italy 1996

Monastery at Simahik

For Colin McNaughton – and dreamers everywhere

WONDER GOAL!

A RED FOX BOOK 0 09 945625 7
First published in Great Britain by Andersen Press Ltd

Andersen Press edition published 2002
Red Fox edition published 2004

3 5 7 9 10 8 6 4 2

Copyright © Michael Foreman, 2002

Red Fox Books are published by Random House Children's Books,
61–63 Uxbridge Road, London W5 5SA,
a division of The Random House Group Ltd,
in Australia by Random House Australia (Pty) Ltd,
20 Alfred Street, Milsons Point, Sydney, NSW 2061, Australia,
in New Zealand by Random House New Zealand Ltd,
18 Poland Road, Glenfield, Auckland 10, New Zealand,
and in South Africa by Random House (Pty) Ltd,
Endulini, 5A Jubilee Road, Parktown 2193, South Africa

THE RANDOM HOUSE GROUP Limited Reg. No. 954009
www.kidsatrandomhouse.co.uk

A CIP catalogue record for this book is available from the British Library.

WONDER GOAL!

MICHAEL FOREMAN

It was a cold Sunday in winter, and the boy hadn't noticed the lads tie his bootlaces together on the way to the game.
So when he tripped and fell out of the builder's van that was their team bus it just made him even more determined to 'show them'.

They were good lads really, but he was new to the team and they always teased the new boy.

And when they ran out to start
the game, he knew they all
dreamed the same dream,
the same impossible dream
of one day becoming
famous footballers.

In the second half, he got his
chance to 'show them'.

It was perfect.
Head over the ball,
balance, power, timing.
All the things his dad
had told him.

As soon as he kicked it,
he knew it was going
to be a goal.
It was a screamer.
No keeper in the world
would save that shot.

Maybe *now* his team mates
would stop teasing him.

Then in his mind,
everything seemed to stop,
frozen in time.

The keeper seemed
to hang in the air,
and the ball hovered
just beyond his fingertips.

It was like a photograph . . .

. . . like all those photographs
that crowded the walls
of his tiny bedroom,
where he dreamed every night
of scoring a wonder goal and
winning the World Cup.

He knew his dad used
to have the same dream
when he was a boy,
and that he too had slept
in a room wall to wall
with heroes.

His dad usually came
to all the games but this
weekend he had to
work overtime.
His dad was not going to
see the wonder goal.
It wouldn't be in the papers
and it wouldn't be on the telly.
And his dad was going to miss it.

All this flashed through
his mind as the ball flew
towards the goal.
And then time clicked
into gear once more
and moved on . . .

and on . . .

The keeper hit the ground . . .

. . . and the ball smacked
into the back of the net.

The vast crowd erupted.
 He had hit another
   wonder goal!

Just like the goal
he had scored all those
years before on that
freezing boyhood Sunday.

Maybe now, after such a goal, his team mates would stop teasing him.
They were good lads really, but he was the newest member of the squad and they always teased the new boy.

And anyway, he knew they had always shared the same dream of winning the World Cup . . .

They hadn't won it yet,
but he *had* just scored
the first goal of the Final . . .
And this time it would
be in all the papers,
and on the telly.

And this time – *this* time,
his dad was there
to see it.